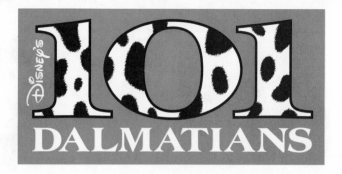

DALMATIANS

Adapted by P. Z. Mann

 A GOLDEN BOOK • NEW YORK

Golden Books Publishing Company, Inc., Racine, Wisconsin 53404

D1511978

A wonderful event had taken place in Roger and Anita's home. Their Dalmatians, Perdy and Pongo, had become parents of fifteen adorable puppies! And though each pup was special, everyone agreed that Fidget was the itchiest, and Wizzer was the bravest.

Anita's boss, the wicked fashion designer Cruella DeVil, also thought the pups were adorable, and tried to buy them. Secretly, though, she really just wanted to make a Dalmatian fur coat! But Roger was suspicious. "They're not for sale," he told her.

"I *must* have those puppies!"
Cruella hissed. She hired two
dim-witted crooks, Horace and
Jasper, to steal them.

While Roger and Anita
were out walking Perdy and
Pongo, the crooks carried off
all fifteen pups in a sack.

Perdy and Pongo were frantic when they found their puppies were gone! Roger and Anita called the police.

Meanwhile, Horace and Jasper drove the puppies over to Cruella's run-down mansion in the country, Manor DeVil.

Desperate to find the puppies, Pongo climbed to the roof and barked out a call for help: *"Woof-woof! Wooooof! Woof! Oooowww!"*

All the dogs who heard him passed on his message until it reached Fogey, a sheepdog on a farm near Manor DeVil.

Fogey called the animals to a meeting in the barn. They were joined by Kipper, an Airedale terrier who had seen the stolen puppies in a truck driving toward the country.

Together, the animals made a plan. Fogey barked a message to Perdy and Pongo, and Kipper went on to Manor DeVil to look for the puppies.

Horace and Jasper didn't notice Kipper sneaking into the mansion. What a mess! Windows were broken, ceilings had fallen, and pipes had burst, leaving everything in shambles.

At last Kipper found Perdy and Pongo's fifteen puppies in the library—along with eighty-four others that Cruella had purchased to make her horrible coat.

Kipper quickly rounded up the ninety-nine puppies and led them toward the attic. Unfortunately, Horace and Jasper spotted them before they had climbed the stairs to safety.

"I don't believe my eyes!" said Jasper. But when the two thieves charged after the pups—CRASH—they fell through a hole in the rotting staircase.

Kipper hurried the puppies up
to the attic and out onto the roof.
Then, one by one, they slid down
the drainpipe to the ground
below. Fogey was waiting there to
lead the puppies back to the barn.

Brave little Wizzer, who was guarding the rear, tricked Jasper into falling through a hole in the floor. And then Wizzer caused Horace to slip, fly out the window, and land in the icy pond!

Pongo and Perdy reached the farm just after Pogey had led the puppies into the barn. They were overjoyed—and very surprised! They hadn't expected to see so many puppies!

By that time Cruella had arrived at her mansion.
"WHERE ARE THE PUPPIES?!" she screamed at Jasper.
Before the crook could explain what had happened, Cruella
discovered a long line of tracks leading from Manor DeVil
toward the farm.

She followed the tracks to the barn. "Come out, little sweetie puppy dogs," Cruella coaxed. But all she found were chickens who pelted her with eggs, and a horse whose powerful kick sent her flying!

Then, from the hayloft, Cruella caught sight of the Dalmatians heading toward the village. They had escaped out the back of the barn. Cruella started to chase them, but suddenly—*GLOP*—she tumbled through a hole in the barn floor right into a vat of molasses!

In the nearby village the police were shocked to see so many Dalmatians.

"I count one hundred, including the two parents," reported a policeman.

Just then Kipper trotted up the road with the last puppy.

"Make that one hundred and one Dalmatians!" the policeman said.

When the police found Cruella, she was a gooey, angry mess. "I'm ruined," she sputtered to Jasper and Horace, "and it's all because you were outsmarted by a pack of puppies!"

But Jasper and Horace, sore and bruised from doing Cruella's dirty work, were glad to be going to jail.

One police car carried Pongo and Perdy's family back to Roger and Anita, followed by a long line of cars bearing the rest of the Dalmatians.

"How on earth can we manage to keep one hundred and one Dalmatians?" wondered Anita.

"We'll work something out," said Roger. "We'll get a bigger place."

And so they did. Manor DeVil needed some fixing up, but it had plenty of room for Roger, Anita, their new baby daughter, and, of course, their one hundred and one Dalmatians!